My Dog Daisy

Jean Ure

With illustrations by
Charlie Alder

First published in 2015 in Great Britain by
Barrington Stoke Ltd
18 Walker Street, Edinburgh, EH3 7LP

www.barringtonstoke.co.uk

Text © 2015 Jean Ure
Illustrations © 2015 Charlie Alder

A CIP catalogue record for this book is available
from the British Library upon request

ISBN: 978-1-78112-496-3

Printed in China by Leo

Contents

Chapter 1
Goldfish

"*I don't want a goldfish!*" I cried.

I didn't want a goldfish. I wanted a dog! Mum knew I wanted a dog. How many times had I begged her?

Mum sighed. "Oh, Lily," she said. "We've been over this so many times."

"But you promised!" I shouted it at her. "You said, when I was 12 I could have one."

"I promised we'd think about it," Mum said.

She'd promised I could have one! Angry tears began to roll down my cheeks. Maybe it's a bit babyish to cry when you're 12 years old, but I had wanted a dog for *such* a long time.

"Gran would have let me," I said.

"Yes. Well." Mum pinched her lips together. "We don't live with your grandmother any more," she said. "I'm sorry, Lily, I know how much you want a dog, but it isn't possible. Not in a small flat with no garden."

'Huh,' I thought. If Mum hadn't fallen out with Gran we wouldn't *be* living in a small flat with no garden. It so wasn't fair!

"To be honest," Mum said, "I'm not even sure we'd be allowed to have a dog here. I think it's against the rules."

"What rules?" I said.

3

Mum looked at me rather hard. She doesn't like it when I speak to her in what she calls "that tone of voice". She says it's rude.

"I don't know why we came here in the first place," I grumbled.

"Lily, you know why we came here," said Mum. "This is what we could afford. Don't be cross with me! I'm doing the best I can. There are all sorts of other pets you could have. How about a hamster? Hamsters are fun."

I didn't want a hamster! I wanted a dog. I wanted one *so much*. I'd wanted one as long as I could remember. Ever since the lady next door to Gran had got a tiny puppy. It was so cute! I used to go and play with it. If only we could have stayed with Gran. It was bad enough that Mum had moved us out – now she wouldn't even let Gran come and visit. She wouldn't even let *me* visit *Gran*. All because they'd had a row.

I snatched up my school bag and banged my way across the kitchen.

"I'm going to school," I said.

"Lily, please don't be like that," Mum said.

For just a moment I hesitated. Maybe I was being unfair. It was true that Gran hadn't always treated Mum very well. And Mum *did* do her best. She was out working all day, looking after other people's gardens for them. Digging and weeding and planting stuff. I knew she would have loved to have a garden of her own.

If we had a garden of our own, I could have my dog.

It was Mum who was being unfair, not me.

"I'm going to meet Keri," I said.

Mum followed me up the hall.

"Don't I even get a goodbye kiss?" she begged.

I gave her a quick, cross peck on the cheek and rushed out. I slammed the door, really hard, behind me.

Chapter 2
More than Anything

Keri and I had been friends for ever. We first met when we were five years old. We did everything together. Told each other everything. No secrets. I knew all about how Keri's dad had lost his job. Keri knew all about why me and Mum didn't live with Gran any more. She also knew how much I wanted a dog. She knew that I wanted a dog more than anything else in the whole wide world.

Keri herself was more of a cat person. She had a big fat furry tabby called Bobbles and she couldn't understand how anyone could prefer dogs, but she tried to be sympathetic. Well, most of the time she did.

"You know what?" she said, as we walked home together after school that day. "You're in a *really* bad mood."

I pulled a face. "It's Mum," I muttered.

"Oh!" Keri rolled her eyes. "Not that again!"

"What do you mean," I said, "*not that again?*" Keri was my best friend! How could she be so unfeeling?

"You were nagging her about a dog," said Keri. "Right?"

I scowled.

"She promised me," I said. "Gran would have let me!"

"Your gran would let you have anything," said Keri. "She'd have let you have the moon if she could have got it for you. That's what my mum says. She says your gran spoiled you rotten and it's no surprise your mum got fed up with it."

"That is so not true!" I said.

"My mum says it is," said Keri.

What did Keri's mum know? I swung my school bag in anger and biffed a lady walking past. She turned and glared at me.

"Sorry," I mumbled.

We walked on in silence for a while.

"You want to know something?" Keri said, at last. "I reckon you're really unkind to your mum."

What a cheek!

"She's unkind to me!" I said. "She won't even let me see my own gran."

I hadn't seen Gran since we'd moved out. That was almost three months ago. Mum didn't even like us talking on the phone.

"At least you've got a gran," Keri said.

Keri didn't have any grandparents at all. But she needn't think I was going to feel sorry for her. How could she be so mean about Gran? All I wanted was my dog.

"Does it have to be a dog?" said Keri. Sometimes it was like she could get into my mind and read what I was thinking. "How about a cat?"

"I don't want a cat!"

"Cats are lovely," Keri said. "They're so clever and cute."

"They don't do anything," I said. "They just lie around sleeping."

"Bobbles doesn't. I play with him! He chases things."

"You can't take him for walks," I said.

"I probably could," said Keri. "If I trained him. Look, I'm just *saying* ... if you can't have a dog, have something else."

"I don't want anything else!" Tears of frustration came spurting into my eyes. I brushed them away before they could spill over down my cheeks. "I don't want a hamster, I don't want a cat, I just want a –"

"How about a guinea pig?" Keri said.

"A GUINEA PIG IS NOT A DOG!"

I screamed it at her. A couple of boys from our class were walking down the road ahead of us. They turned to stare. I groaned. Robbie Baxter, and his mate Ryan Goff! *Yuck.* They both grinned. Robbie cupped a hand to his ear.

"Say again, Lily," he shouted. "Didn't quite catch that!"

"Go away!" I yelled.

They shambled off, still grinning.

"*Idiots*," I said.

"Well, you asked for it," said Keri. "Screeching like that."

"I'm just sick of people telling me that guinea pigs and hamsters are as good as dogs!"

"I was only trying to help," Keri said. "If you don't *want* to be helped –"

"I don't!"

"In that case," she said, "I might as well go." She raised a hand. "See you."

Keri marched off towards her bus stop. I was left on my own, with the tears starting to well up again in my eyes. Nobody understood how miserable I was. Not even my best friend.

Chapter 3
Fred

I always walked home across the park. It was only a small park, just a patch of grass with a path going round it, but there was an old stone water fountain in the middle, and a pond with ducks. Best of all, lots of people walked their dogs there. Sometimes, if I was lucky, I got to talk to one.

I talked to dogs whenever I could. I played with them, too. Last week I'd kicked a ball for a big sloppy Labrador who got over-excited and jumped up at me with his great dirty paws. I was covered in mud. His owner was horrified, but I wasn't bothered. I told her that I loved dogs. What did a bit of mud matter?

Today I could see the Labrador in the distance. He seemed to be the only dog in the park. He was going out the far gate. I had missed him!

I shambled on, round the path. I was almost at the gate when I saw an old lady sitting on a bench. I'd seen her before, over the other side of the park. She had a small black dog that pottered about on shaky legs. Today the dog was curled up beside her on the bench. I stopped.

"Is it all right if I talk to him?" I said. You always have to ask, just in case.

The old lady smiled. "He would love you to talk to him. There's nothing he enjoys more than a bit of a chat."

I giggled. The old lady patted the bench for me to take a seat.

"Some people," she said, "don't realise that you can have a chat with a dog."

"I love having chats with dogs," I said. I sat down and held out a hand, with the palm upwards to show him I was friendly. He nosed at it and his tail began to thump.

"There," the old lady said. "He likes you."

Dogs always like me. They can tell when you are a dog person.

"What shall I talk to him about?" I said.

"That's up to you," the old lady said. "His name, by the way, is Fred."

I said, "How do you do, Fred?" I took his paw. "I'm Lily."

"And I'm Charlotte," the old lady said. "There! Now we have all been introduced. Now we can talk. Do you have a dog of your own, Lily?"

"No!" The tears sprang back into my eyes. "My mum won't let me. She says we can't, cos we live in a flat."

"I live in a flat too," Charlotte said. "Just over there." She pointed, across the park. "But I have a garden. Don't you have one?"

"No, but my gran does," I said. "I *could* have had a dog if Mum hadn't gone and moved us out. Gran would have let me. Now I don't even see her any more."

"That's a shame," said Charlotte.

I bent over and rubbed my face in Fred's fur. He smelled all doggy in a nice sort of way.

"Mum wants me to get a hamster," I said.

Charlotte nodded. "But you want a dog."

"I'm a dog sort of person," I told her.

"I can see that," Charlotte said. "Maybe you could share Fred with me."

I sprang up. "Really?"

Did she mean it?

"We are always in the park at about this time," said Charlotte. "We used to walk all the way round but our legs aren't too good any more, so now we just have a bit of a toddle then come and sit down. It would make Fred very happy if you joined us."

"I could even take him for a toddle," I said.

"You could," Charlotte said. "He'd enjoy that. So long as your mum doesn't mind."

"I'm sure she won't," I said. Why would Mum mind? She was always out working. She almost never arrived home before 5 o'clock. I would have lots of time to take Fred for his toddle.

"Oh, look, he's trying to get into my bag!" I said. "Maybe he wants to do some of my homework for me."

Charlotte gave a little chuckle. "I don't think so! More likely he can smell food in there."

I opened my bag and me and Fred peered in together.

"KitKat!" I said. Fred's nose quivered. "Can he have a piece?"

Charlotte shook her head. "Not chocolate," she said. "Chocolate is very bad for dogs."

"Oh." My heart sank. "That's all I've got. Maybe tomorrow I could bring him a treat? A special dog treat."

"He loves treats," Charlotte said. "So long as it's a nice soft one. I'm afraid his poor old teeth aren't what they used to be. He's not a young man any more."

I could see now that Fred's muzzle was almost totally white, just like Charlotte's hair. Even my gran's hair wasn't white. Charlotte must be *really* old. Fred, too. But he could still go for a toddle!

"Bye bye, Freddy." I dropped a kiss on top of his head. "I'll see you tomorrow!"

Chapter 4
Friends Again

"I hope we're friends again," Keri said, as we walked back together after school the next day.

"Of course we are," I said.

It wasn't like we'd had a proper row or anything. We'd just had a bit of a falling-out. It's what friends do! It doesn't mean you stop being friends. But I told her that I was sorry, cos I felt maybe I'd been a bit mean.

"You were in ever such a mood," said Keri.

"I know." I was about to swing my bag but remembered just in time what had happened yesterday. "Sometimes you can't help it," I said. "Things get to you."

"Like how you aren't allowed to have a dog." Keri nodded, kindly. "I expect I'd be in a mood if I couldn't have a cat. Specially Bobbles. He is so-o-o sweet! Do you know what he did last night? He –" She broke off. "Where are you going? You're going the wrong way."

"I'm going to the pet shop," I said. "I have to buy some dog treats."

"*Dog* treats?" Keri said.

"For a dog," I said.

"But you haven't got a dog!"

"I'm sharing one," I said. "D'you want to come and see?"

It was a mistake, taking Keri to meet Fred. She is so not a dog person. Fred was every bit as sweet as her Bobbles, but she just couldn't see it. All she could see was an old grey dog.

He was so pleased with his treat. It was a nice soft chewy one, and he held it between his paws as he munched on it.

"That is so clever," I said. "He's using his paws like hands."

"Bobbles does that," said Keri.

"Bobbles can't go for walks," I said. "Fred can. Can't he?" I turned to Charlotte. "Can he come for a walk?"

"He can if you don't mind going at his pace," said Charlotte. "I'm afraid he can't do much more than potter, these days."

"I like pottering," I said.

We pottered together up the path, me and Fred in the sunshine. Keri pottered with us for a bit, then said she had to go.

"We'll come with you as far as the gate," I said.

I could tell she didn't really want us to. Keri is quite an impatient sort of person. Every time Fred stopped to sniff at something she made a little huffing sound and pulled a face.

"He can't help it," I said. "It's what old dogs do."

In the end I told her to go. I almost wished I hadn't invited her. I was so proud of sharing Fred. I didn't care if his muzzle was white and his legs were wobbly and his teeth not as good as they had been. He was my dog. Well, partly my dog.

I didn't say anything to Mum about him – it seemed best not to. Mum gets a bit stressed,

sometimes. Like for ages she fussed about me walking home from school by myself. She even said maybe she should give up one of her gardening jobs so she could come and collect me. I had to point out that I was in high school now.

It still didn't stop Mum worrying. I could just hear her.

"Lily, who is this Charlotte person?" she'd say. "What do you know about her?"

Or, even worse – "Lily, I don't want you walking through that park any more."

If I couldn't walk in the park, I wouldn't see Fred. I couldn't bear it! It would break my heart if I had to stop seeing Fred. So I didn't say a word and Mum never knew what it was that was making me so happy all of a sudden.

But if I had a secret, Mum had one too.

Chapter 5
Secret

I surprised Mum on the phone one evening a few weeks later.

I didn't mean to listen. I was supposed to be in my room doing homework and Mum was in the kitchen. I was on my way there in search of something to eat (doing homework makes you really hungry), when I heard Mum talking.

I heard her say, "Yes, these last few weeks she's been so much calmer. I think she's accepted at last that we simply *can't* have a d–"

And then she saw me standing in the door and her face went bright red. "Listen, I'm going to have to go," she said. "We'll speak soon!"

"Who was that?" I said.

"Nobody," said Mum. "Why aren't you doing your homework?"

"I was," I said. "I am! I got hungry."

"Well, have a glass of milk," said Mum, "and get back to it."

She looked really guilty.

"Was that a boyfriend?" I said.

"*Lily.*" She almost shouted it. ('Definitely guilty,' I thought.) "Just go and get on with your homework."

"No, but was it?" I said.

"Questions, questions!" said Mum. She pointed at the door. "Go!"

I went.

But the next day I said to Keri that I reckoned Mum had a secret boyfriend who she didn't want me to know about.

"What makes you think that?" said Keri.

"Cos she couldn't get off the phone fast enough," I said. "*And* she was all red."

"Wow." I could see Keri turning it over in her mind. "Would it bother you?" she said.

"Dunno." I crinkled my nose. "I'd rather have Gran back."

"At least you've got your dog," said Keri.

"Ye-e-es," I said. "I suppose."

"Well, you have!" Keri sounded a bit impatient, like, *Oh, there she goes again.* "What's the matter now?"

I didn't tell her cos I didn't want her to say I was always complaining, but I was starting to get worried about Fred. The last two days he hadn't wanted to go for his toddle round the park. Yesterday I'd brought him a squeaky toy, but he hadn't even looked up when I squeaked it at him.

I told Keri that I was just feeling a bit down.

"Is it cos of your mum?" she said. "Having a boyfriend?"

"Could be," I said.

"He might be OK," Keri said. "You might like him."

"Mm ... maybe," I said.

"Well, you might," Keri said. "You never know. There's my bus, I gotta go. See you tomorrow!"

Keri ran off towards the bus stop while I turned and went into the park. For a moment I couldn't see any sign of Charlotte and Fred. A kind of panic came over me. Where were they? And then Charlotte waved at me from the far side, and I raced towards her across the grass.

"Hello, Fred!" I sank down beside him, but for once he didn't wag his tail.

"He's not feeling too chipper," Charlotte said. "He didn't have a very good night. I'm afraid we have to face it, Lily … his time may be coming."

I didn't ask her what she meant. I think I sort of knew. I just didn't want her to say it.

"Look!" I cried. "He's trying to get into my bag!"

Charlotte gave a sad little smile. "You must have something nice in there."

"Only chocolate," I said. "Naughty Fred!" I rubbed my cheek into his fur. "Chocolate isn't good for dogs."

"Today," Charlotte said, "it doesn't matter. Today he can have whatever he wants."

I looked at her, shocked. "You said chocolate's bad for him."

"Not today," said Charlotte. "Today is special. Let him have his chocolate. It will be a happy memory."

I broke off a square and held it out. Fred's nose quivered over it for a moment.

"Oh," I cried, "he doesn't want it!"

Something wet dropped onto my hand. I looked up to find Charlotte dabbing her eyes. Old people did that. They were always dabbing their eyes. It didn't mean they were crying.

"Fred's *such* a good boy," I said. "He knows he shouldn't have chocolate. He wants it really."

"What he wants more than anything," Charlotte said, "is to have a good long rest."

I nodded. "Then when he wakes up he'll feel better."

Charlotte was silent.

"He will," I said, "won't he?"

"Fred will be at peace," said Charlotte. "And now, Lily, I think I must take him home. Do you want to say goodbye to him?"

I pressed my lips against his face.

"Bye bye, Fred!" I whispered. "Sleep tight!"

Chapter 6
Sleep Tight

When I walked into the park the next day, I thought that Fred would be there. I thought that he and Charlotte would be sitting on the bench, the same as always. Fred would wag, and Charlotte would smile. "He's had a nice long rest," she would say. "He's feeling lots better."

But Charlotte was all by herself. There was no little black dog curled up next to her.

"Lily," she said. She patted the bench beside her. "Come and sit with me."

We sat for a while in silence.

Then, very gently, Charlotte said, "It was time, Lily. For his sake."

I felt my eyes begin to prick.

"He fell asleep so easily," said Charlotte.

"When he wakes up –" I blotted my eyes on the back of my sleeve. "If you're not there ... won't he be lonely?"

"Fred won't be lonely," said Charlotte. "He'll be playing in the sunshine with all his old friends. All the dogs he has known. They'll all be there together." She sighed. "I'll be the one who's lonely. I miss him so much."

"So do I," I said, and I could hear my voice was all shaky.

Charlotte's hand closed over mine. "We must both try to be brave, Lily." And then she took something from her pocket and held it out. "This is for you. To remember him by."

It was Fred's collar. The little tartan collar that he had always worn.

"I'll keep it for ever!" I said.

I did try really hard to be brave. But it was oh-so painful. Before I'd met Fred, I had been angry and miserable. Now I was just sad. Sad, sad, *sad*.

I didn't want to walk in the park any more and talk to other dogs. I didn't want other dogs. I wanted Fred. I didn't think of poor Charlotte, all by herself.

"Has something happened?" Keri said.

I had to tell her, she's my best friend. You can't keep things from your best friend.

Keri was so good! She put her arm round me and gave me a hug.

"He was such a sweet little dog," she said.

I nearly broke down, when Keri said that. Keri, who wasn't even a dog person. I did my very best to be brave, but I couldn't stop the tears coming. Before I knew it, they were rolling in rivers down my cheeks.

Just my luck that those two stupid boys, Robbie Baxter and Ryan Goff, happened to be walking past. Them, of all people!

"What's her problem?" Ryan said. "What's she blubbing about?"

"Do you mind?" Keri screamed. "She's just lost her dog!"

"*Lost* it?" Ryan said. "Where's it gone?"

He probably thought he was being funny. Or maybe he really didn't understand. After all, I hadn't at first. I hadn't been brave enough to face the truth.

Keri opened her mouth to say something, but Robbie got in first. He poked Ryan in the ribs. "Shut up!" he said. And then he turned to me. His face had gone a bit pink. "Sorry about your dog," he mumbled. "My sister lost her guinea pig last week."

Robbie walked off, dragging Ryan with him.

"Guinea pig!" said Keri. "It's hardly the same as losing a dog. Those boys are such idiots!"

I agreed that Ryan was. Ryan was a total idiot. I wasn't so sure about Robbie. Maybe he wasn't so bad. After all, he had tried.

The next morning, Mum noticed I wasn't happy.

"Oh, Lily," she said. "I was hoping you'd got over all that."

I could have said, "Got over all what?" – but I didn't. I just pulled the duvet round my head and squeezed my eyes tight shut. I knew what Mum was thinking. She was thinking, 'Lily is sulking again.'

"Sweetheart," Mum said. "You know we can't have a dog. Not in a 5th-floor flat. Come on! Make a bit of an effort, there's a good girl. You can't stay in bed all day. It's Saturday morning and the sun is shining. Why don't we go over to the park and feed the ducks? You used to love feeding the ducks."

"That was when I was little," I muttered.

"Well, let's pretend you're still little," Mum said. "Let's go and have some fun!"

But I wouldn't. I felt that I never wanted to go over to the park ever again. Not without Fred.

Chapter 7
12 o'Clock Sharp

Monday was half-term and I'd arranged to meet up with Keri to help her buy a birthday present for her mum. We always helped each other buy presents. It was part of the fun.

"We're just going to look round the shops," I told Mum. "Is that OK?"

I'd thought Mum would be pleased. I wasn't lying in bed! I'd got up before she'd had to come and yell at me. I was going out with my best friend. I was *making an effort*. But Mum frowned. She didn't seem very pleased at all.

"Mum?" I said. "Is it OK?"

"So long as you're back here by 12," said Mum. "Not a minute later."

"But that only gives us two hours!" I wailed.

"Plenty of time to find a present," said Mum. And then, as she saw me off in the lift, she reminded me *again*. "12 o'clock sharp!"

"I don't know why she wants me back that early," I grumbled, as Keri and I set off for the shops.

"Didn't you ask her?" said Keri.

"No." I pulled a face. "I was scared she wouldn't let me come at all. What are you going to get for your mum?"

"I'm going to get her an ornament," Keri said. "A little cat ornament! I saw –"

She broke off as a familiar voice shouted at us from a side street. "Oi! You two!"

Keri groaned. "Not *them* again."

She meant Robbie and Ryan. But it was only Robbie, by himself. He came charging towards us.

"What do you want?" said Keri.

"Got something for you," said Robbie. "For *her*."

"You mean Lily?" said Keri. "She does have a name, you know."

"Yeah. Lily!" Robbie nodded. "She likes dogs. I've got one for her."

"If this is some kind of stupid joke ..." Keri said.

"It's not a joke," said Robbie. "Honest! Come and have a look."

"Ignore him," said Keri. She linked her arm with mine. "Let's go and get Mum's present."

I hesitated. "Is there really a dog?" I said.

"Of course there isn't!" Keri's voice was scornful. "He's just having you on."

"I'm not," said Robbie. "There *is* a dog. Scruffy little thing. Needs someone to take care of it."

"Why?" said Keri. "Where's its owners?"

"Gone," said Robbie. "Weeks ago. They used to live next door to us, then one day they just moved out and left it. I asked my mum if we could have it, but she said no. It's kind of

48

scabby-looking. They never did look after it right."

"Oh!" I tore my arm away from Keri's.

"What are you doing?" Keri shrieked.

"I'm going to go and look!" I said.

I set off down the street with Robbie. After a bit of huffing and puffing, Keri followed.

"Don't blame me when it turns out to be some sort of stupid joke," she said.

But it wasn't a stupid joke. There really was a dog.

Chapter 8
Tomorrow

"What did I tell you?" said Robbie.

A tiny black dog was peering at us with big frightened eyes from behind a row of bins.

"It looks a bit like Fred," said Keri.

I was thinking the same thing myself.

"Poor little girl!" I crouched down by the bins, and held out my hand.

"Careful it doesn't bite you," said Keri.

"She won't bite," I said. "Her tail's wagging." I turned to Robbie. "What's her name? Do you know?"

"I think it's Daisy," said Robbie. "That's what I heard them call her."

"Daisy!" She had come creeping up to me and was snuffling in my hand. "She's hungry," I said.

"Yeah," Robbie said. "I reckon they never fed her enough. You gonna take her, or what?"

Keri turned to look at me.

Daisy also looked at me. Her eyes were big and sad, but full of hope.

"Yes," I said. "I'm taking her!"

"We haven't got a lead," Keri said.

"Here." Robbie had bent down and was busy unlacing his trainers. I started unlacing mine, as well. "Tie 'em all together," said Robbie. "All the laces … there you go!"

"She hasn't got a collar," Keri said.

"I've got a collar," I said. I had Fred's collar in my pocket. I'd been carrying it everywhere, in memory of Fred. I felt sure he wouldn't mind me using it to help a poor little lost dog.

"I reckon she'll be OK now," Robbie said. "Been on her own for weeks, she has." And then he hesitated. "If you were gonna keep her," he said, "I could always help take her for walks."

He'd gone bright pink! "Really?" I said. "D'you mean it?"

"Yeah, why not?" said Robbie. "I like dogs."

With that, he turned and ran off. I thought to myself that he *wasn't* such a bad sort of boy.

Keri and I walked back the way we had come, with Daisy on her lead and me slipping and slopping in my loose trainers.

"You know, don't you," said Keri, "your mum's never going to let you keep her?"

"I know." It was a bit of a worry. Mum had shown me the letter from the landlord where it said in big letters, "NO DOGS ALLOWED."

"So what are you going to do?" said Keri. "Take her to the police?"

"No!" I shook my head, fiercely.

I had a plan. If it didn't work out then maybe I *would* have to take Daisy to the police or the dogs' home. But I really didn't want to! They would put her in a cage, and she would be so unhappy.

"I'm going to find a home for her." I turned back, towards the park. "I'm really sorry about

your mum's present," I said, "but Daisy needs our help."

Keri sighed, but she didn't argue.

"It's OK," she said. "I'll come with you."

The park was almost empty. There was just a woman with two red setters down at the far end. No sign of Charlotte. But I had Fred's collar. I squatted down to read the address on the metal tag attached to it.

Fred Miller, it said. *Flat 1B, Fairfield Court.*

Fairfield Court was the big block on the other side of the park. Daisy and I set off towards it. Keri hopped and skipped at our side.

"Where are we going?" she said. "Where are we going?"

"We're going to see Charlotte," I said.

Chapter 9
Daisy, Daisy!

"Lily!" Charlotte looked very surprised to see us. "Come in, come in!"

Me and Daisy walked into the hall. Keri followed.

"So, you've got a dog at last," Charlotte said. "I'm so pleased! I know how much you wanted one. Bring her in! Let me see her."

"She's a bit scruffy," I said.

I told Charlotte how her horrible owners had moved out and left her behind, and how Robbie had saved her.

"What a very nice young man he must be," Charlotte said. "And what a dear little dog! But oh dear, she is very thin. She must be starving."

"She's been living on the street for simply ages," I said.

"In that case," said Charlotte, "we must feed her. What is her name?"

"Daisy," I said.

"Here we are then, Daisy." Charlotte opened a cupboard and took out a tin of dog food. I saw that she had lots of other tins in there. She filled a bowl and Daisy ate and ate.

"Poor little soul," said Charlotte, as she sat on the sofa. "I can see all her ribs! But we mustn't give her too much in one go. I'll put the rest of these tins in a bag for you to take with you."

I hesitated. Keri looked at me and frowned. I sat down next to Charlotte and watched as Daisy cleaned up every last bit of food from her bowl. When she had finished, she walked across the room, jumped onto the sofa, gave a big happy sigh and settled herself down next to Charlotte.

I held my breath. Some people don't like dogs on the furniture. Maybe Charlotte would be cross and tell her off. But she didn't. She just put an arm round her so that Daisy could snuggle closer.

"Well, she certainly enjoyed that," Charlotte said. "You must feed her again, Lily, when you get her back home."

"I can't!" The words came bursting out of me. "I can't take her back with me!"

"Her mum won't let her," said Keri.

"We're not allowed to." My top lip had begun to tremble. Was I going to have to take that poor little dog to the police station after all? I looked at Charlotte. She and Daisy were cuddled up really close. "I was hoping maybe you could take her," I whispered.

"Me?" Charlotte said. "Oh, Lily! There is nothing I would love more. But, my dear, I'm too old. I couldn't give her the exercise she needs."

"I could!" I sprang forward on the sofa. "I could stop by every morning on my way to school and every afternoon on my way home. You could bring her to the park and I could walk round with her. We could share her," I said. "Like we shared Fred."

There was a long silence.

Then Daisy did this really sweet thing. She stretched out a paw and laid it on Charlotte's knee. Charlotte looked down at her. I held my breath. Were those tears in Charlotte's eyes? I should never have said Fred's name. How could I be so unfeeling? Poor Charlotte.

And then I realised ... she was smiling! A little trembly smile. But still a smile.

"Daisy, Daisy!" Charlotte shook her head. "What can I say? It seems she's here to stay. But she'll still be your dog, Lily."

My dog. My dog Daisy! My heart swelled. It was only then that I remembered. Mum wanted me home no later than 12.

"I have to go now," I said. "But I'll come back this afternoon to take her for a walk."

"She'll be waiting for you," Charlotte promised.

Chapter 10
A Big Surprise

I ran all the way home from Charlotte's, but I still arrived ten minutes late.

"Lily!" Mum said, as she opened the door. "What did I tell you?"

"I couldn't help it," I said. "Something happened! Something really important!"

"Yes, well, this is something really important, too," said Mum. "You have a visitor.

A very special visitor. You remember you accused me of having a boyfriend?"

'Oh no,' I thought. 'Please!'

I wanted Mum to be happy, but I really didn't want her having a boyfriend. Not right now. Maybe in a little while.

Mum must have seen my face fall.

"You see?" said Mum. "This is what comes when you listen to other people's conversations. You get hold of the wrong end of the stick. Go on in!" She gave me a little push towards the sitting room. "Go and give your gran a kiss."

"Gran!" I cried. I hurled myself forward into her arms. "Gran, I've got a dog!"

"A dog?" said Gran. "Have you really?"

"What dog is this?" said Mum.

"Her name's Daisy," I said, "and I'm sharing her cos I know she can't come and live here. But I'm going to take her for walks every day with my friend Robbie, and she is just *so sweet*, I know you'll love her!"

And then I got a bit worried, and I stopped and turned to Mum.

"Mum, I can bring her here just to show you," I said. "Can't I?"

"Of course you can," said Mum. "But who are you sharing her with?"

"Charlotte," I said. "Mum, she's this old lady I met in the park. She had this dear little dog called Fred and I used to take him for toddles, cos he was too old to walk very far. And then he died and poor Charlotte was so sad, and I was sad, too. But then I found Daisy and gave her to Charlotte. So now she's got Daisy and she said I can share her and take her for walks.

And sometimes bring her back here just to say hello?"

Mum seemed a bit confused. "I think maybe I should say hello to Charlotte, as well," she said.

"Oh," I cried, "that's a good idea! She could come when I bring Daisy. Oh, and Mum," I said, "can Gran be here, too?"

I did so want to show Daisy to Gran!

"Don't worry," said Mum. "Your gran will be here. We'll all be here."

My heart swelled. Me, and Mum, and Gran ... and my dog Daisy!

Our books are tested
for children and young people by
children and young people.

Thanks to everyone who consulted on
a manuscript for their time and effort in
helping us to make our books better
for our readers.